WHERE THE Sunrise Begins

WORDS BY *Douglas Wood*

ART BY *Wendy Popp*

Simon & Schuster Books for Young Readers

NEW YORK   LONDON   TORONTO   SYDNEY

The world is always turning,
turning toward the dawn.
And although nights can be dark and long,
each day brings a brand new sunrise.

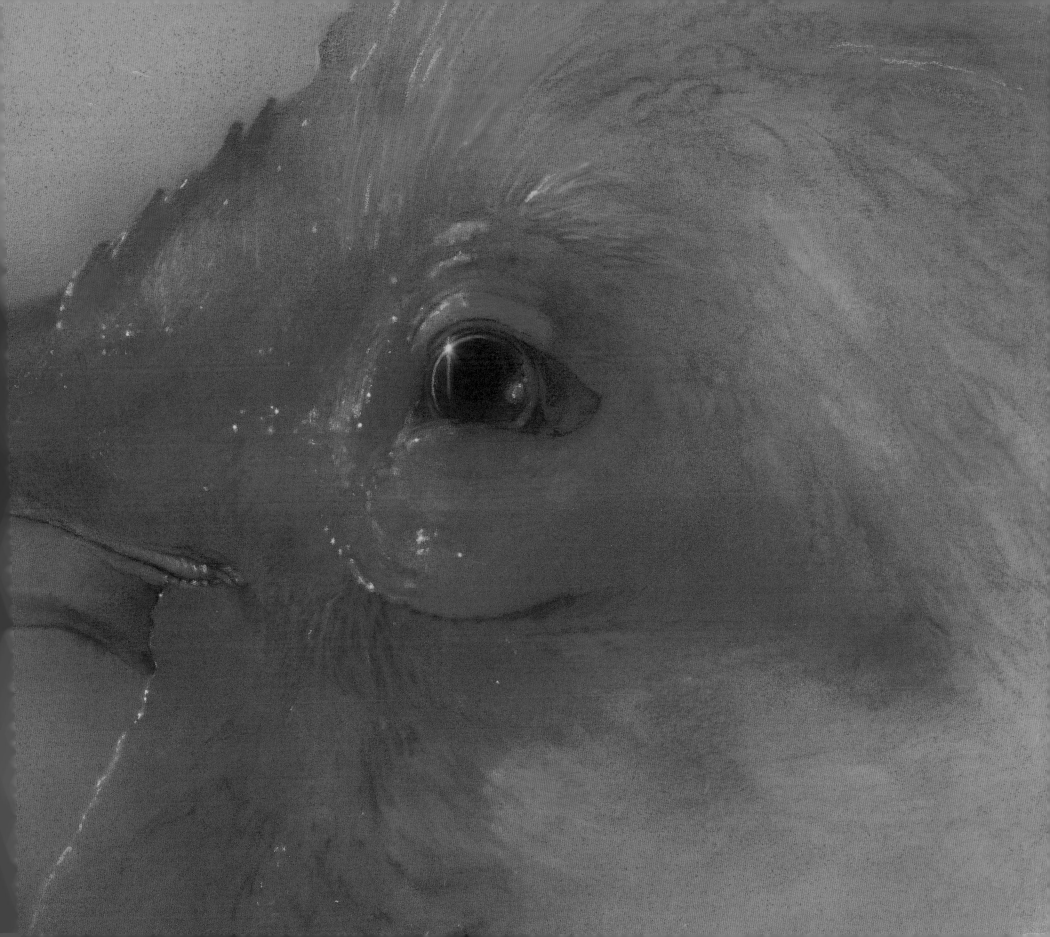

But where does the sunrise begin?

Some say it begins on the mountain,
    so high above the earth
    that you can see the sunlight before it ever touches
    rivers or lakes or forests or prairies,
    all lying far below.
    Here the first morning candle
    burns away the darkness.

But the mountain is not
where the sunrise begins.

Some say it begins in the treetop,
    where the birds notice the first soft light
    and begin to sing,
    each in their own way,
    with their own melody,
    waking the sleepy world around them,
    while the first breeze shivers the smallest leaves.

But the treetop is not
where the sunrise begins.

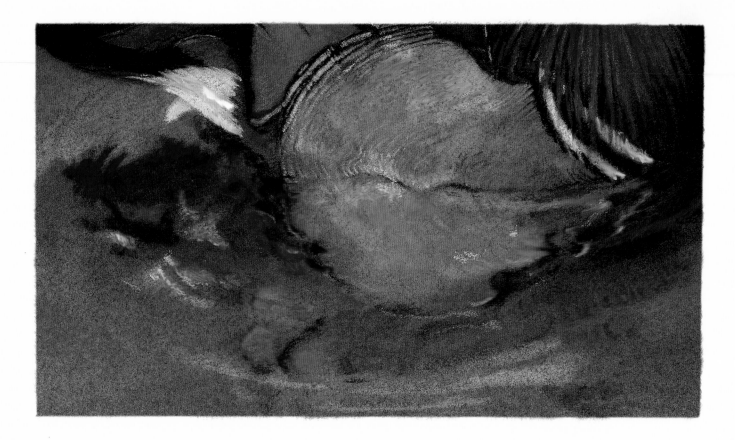

Some say it begins in the marsh,
    where drowsy ducks
       shake their heads and fluff their feathers
       and test their wings for the day's first flight,
       and speak in soft, murmuring tones about
       the things that ducks know,
       while the muskrat glides silently through the cattails.
But the marsh is not where the sunrise begins.

Some say it begins on the lake,
	where fish rise and dimple
	the smooth, glassy surface;
	where the water rises and falls as if breathing,
	and chuckles in the hollow places
	along the rocky shore,
	and someone on a dock plops in the first bobber of the day.

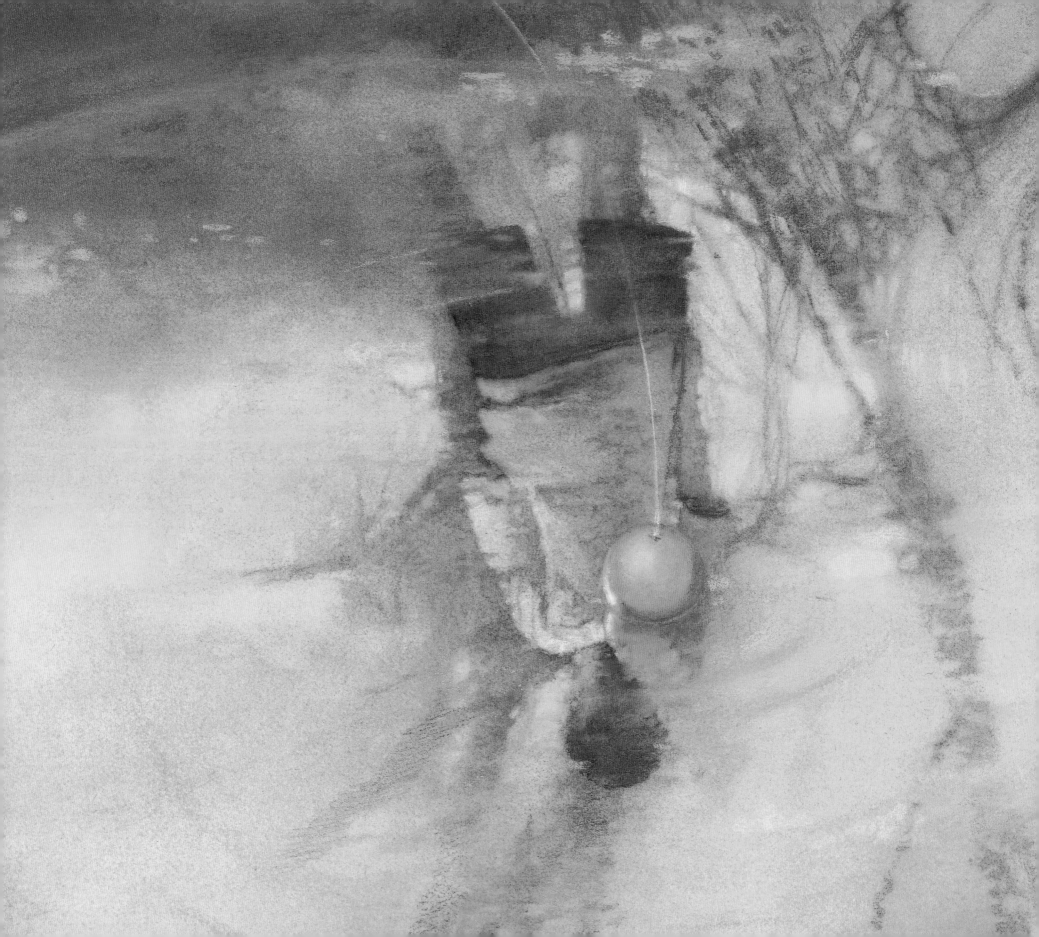

But the lake is not
where the sunrise begins.

Some say it starts upon the great, rolling sea,
    over waters deeper than the highest mountains,
    on oceans that enfold and encircle all the earth
    and make life itself possible;
    where ships have long sailed into the great unknown
    and where travelers know the ancient saying,
    "Red sky at morning, sailors take warning,"
But the sea is not where the sunrise begins.

Some say it begins in Africa,
  where life first arose and walked on two legs
  and spoke its own name;
  where the bones of a being who lived
  a thousand million sunrises ago
  wait for the sun, and for someone to find them,
  and learn their ancient story.

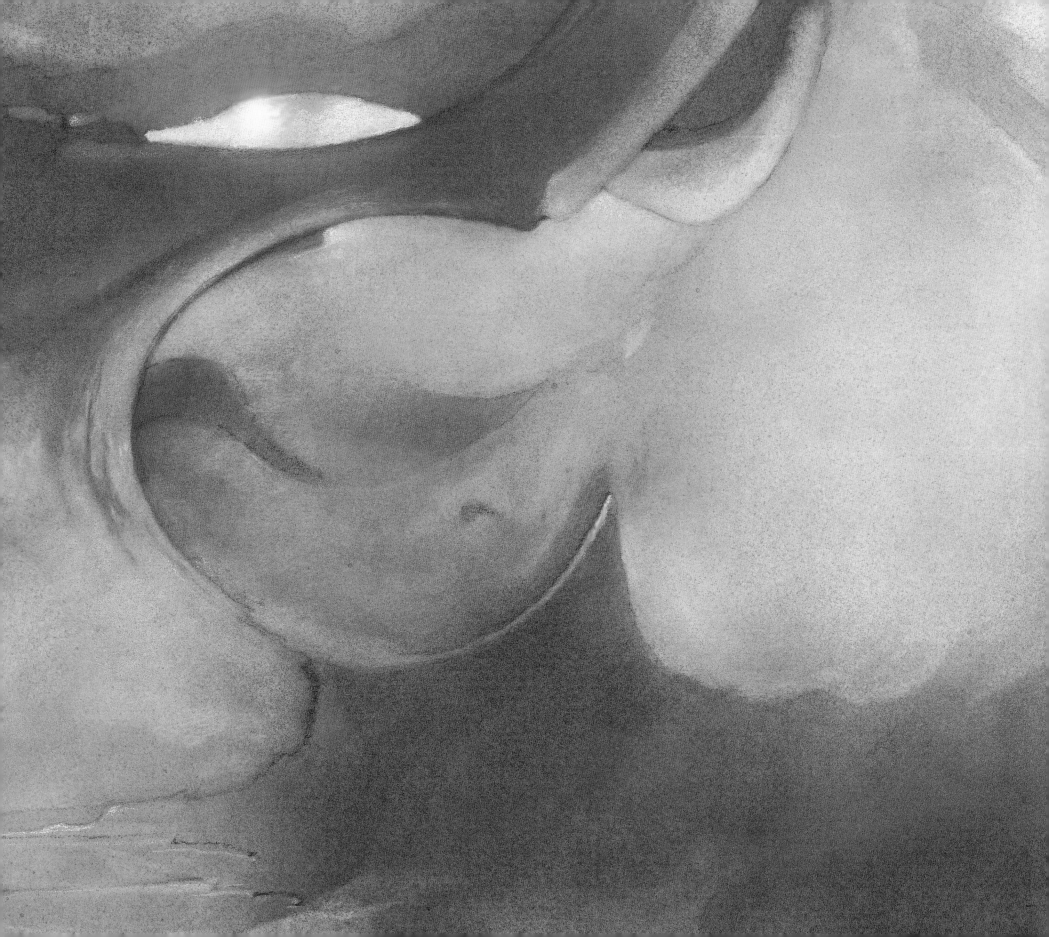

But Africa is not where the sunrise begins.

Some say it begins in the Far East,
    the "Land of the Rising Sun,"
    where people have long greeted the day
    with prayer and meditation
    and the sound of a gong;
    where the sky blooms with the first light
    and bonsai trees cradle the sun upon tiny branches.

But the Far East is not
where the sunrise begins.

Some say it begins in the Middle East,
    where the light of many great religions first shone;
    where Abraham and Moses
    and Mohammed and Jesus walked
    and listened for a still, small voice,
    a voice that people argue over yet today,
    in a land known as Holy.
But the Middle East is not where the sunrise begins.

Some say it begins in our own native land,
    where the first light falls upon
    scenes that are known and loved;
    where people speak a familiar language
    and act in familiar ways,
    and where the rest of the world
    seems a bit strange and far away.

But our native land is not
where the sunrise begins.

Then where does the sunrise begin?

Because the world is always turning toward morning,
every moment brings the sunrise to someone,
somewhere in the world.
Wherever there is a heart that loves the light,
that holds a place for hope,
and feels gratitude for each new day,
in that heart the sun is always rising
and helping to fill the world with light.
Where *does* the sunrise begin?

The sunrise begins in you.

To Eric James, Bryan Douglas, and Kathy Ann, and to all who share the light—D. W.

To Wynn, who always shares his luminous heart,
and to Neda, whose last light will illuminate dark corners around the earth—W. P.

Acknowledgments

Warm thanks to my editor, Emily Meehan, who guided
this project to fruition. To Wendy, for inspired art that
exceeded my imagination. To Chloë, for careful attention
that gives that last touch of grace. And especially to my
wife, Kathy, who helps prepare every book.—D. W.

It has been a special privilege to collaborate with Doug
Wood to create a book filled with light. In many ways,
honoring the text has shed light in many corners of my
own studio. It reflects back in the gentle faces of Rebecca
S., Grace D., Araad A. S., and of course, Wynn S. I would
like to thank the children for generously sharing their
personal glow for the characters in these pages. To Justin
and Emily, my gratitude, for a brilliant opportunity. To
gracious Chloë, appreciation for your patience.—W. P.

SIMON & SCHUSTER BOOKS FOR YOUNG READERS • An imprint of Simon & Schuster Children's Publishing Division • 1230 Avenue of the Americas, New York, New York 10020
Text copyright © 2010 by Douglas Wood, Inc. • Illustrations copyright © 2010 by K. Wendy Popp • All rights reserved, including the right of reproduction in whole or in part in any form.
SIMON & SCHUSTER BOOKS FOR YOUNG READERS is a trademark of Simon & Schuster, Inc. • For information about special discounts for bulk purchases, please contact Simon & Schuster Special
Sales at 1-866-506-1949 or business@simonandschuster.com. • The Simon & Schuster Speakers Bureau can bring authors to your live event. For more information or to book an event, contact
the Simon & Schuster Speakers Bureau at 1-866-248-3049 or visit our website at www.simonspeakers.com. • Book design by Chloë Foglia • The text for this book is set in Stempel Schneidler
Std. The illustrations for this book are rendered in conté crayon and pastel. The artist worked from life and referred to her own photographs whenever possible. She has taken great pleasure
in including friends and family members among the faces in this work. This is the first time that her drawings have been darkened digitally. • Manufactured in China • 0210 KWO
10 9 8 7 6 5 4 3 2 1 • Library of Congress Cataloging-in-Publication Data • Wood, Douglas, 1951– • Where the sunrise begins / Douglas Wood ; illustrated by Wendy Popp. — 1st ed.
p. cm. • Summary: Reveals the part that each of us plays in the beginning of every day. • ISBN 978-0-689-86172-7 (hardcover) • [1. Sun—Rising and setting—Fiction. 2. Nature—Fiction.]
I. Popp, Wendy, ill. II. Title. • PZ7.W84738Wk 2010 • [E]—dc22 • 2009040647

16.99

7/10

QBI